for Karen Sartain

who doesn't just plant seeds,
but waters them too.

Curious
Carmelita

written by Patricia McFadden

illustrated by Robin McFadden

Published in the United States by Green Turtle Press,
an imprint of Green Turtle Arts. Please visit
http:\\greenturtlearts.com

Carmelita and her family live near the Mexican border, so they use many Spanish words. Here is a glossary of Spanish words from the book:

abuela—grandmother

abuelo—grandfather

chiquita--little one

gracias--thank you

hermana—sister

mamacita---mother

por favor--please

prima--cousin

senorita--miss

si—yes

tia – aunt

In a hidden valley high in the southern mountains of Arizona there lived a band of coatimundis. They all had white markings on their faces, tapered snouts, strong claws and long, striped tails that stuck straight up in the air. All, that is, except the smallest coatimundi, Carmelita. Instead of sticking straight up, Carmelita's tail curved like a question mark. Her *Mamacita* said this was because Carmelita was so curious.

All day, every day, Carmelita asked questions.

"Why do elegant trogon birds have red breasts?" she asked her Mamacita.

"Why do king snakes and coral snakes look so much alike?" she asked her *tia* Louisa.

"Why does our water seep never dry up?" she asked her *prima* Maria.

"Why is a prickly pear cactus prickly?" she asked her *hermana* Lucia.

All day, every day, she got the same answer. "Not now, Carmelita! I'm too busy to answer questions. Go ask *Abuela*!"

Abuela was very old. Her tail stripes were gray with age. Her joints ached and her claws were blunt. She could no longer hunt for food.

Each morning, Abuela climbed stiffly down from her favorite sleeping perch in the crook of a sycamore tree. Slowly, she made her way to the water seep. Once there, she sat and warmed her old bones in the sun as one of the kits brought her sweet grubs or juicy berries for breakfast.

"*Gracias*," Abuela always said, then asked, "would you like to hear a story?"

Maria or Lucia replied, "not now, Abuela. I'm too busy."

But Carmelita always answered, "*Si*, Abuela. I love your stories."

Carmelita and Abuela sat together and groomed each other's fur while Abuela told stories and Carmelita asked questions.

"Carmelita should spend less time sitting with Abuela and more time hunting for food like the rest of us!" Tia Louisa scolded.

"Leave them alone, Louisa," Mamacita replied. "They need each other."

"Hmph!" snorted Tia Louisa. But she left them alone.

There was one story Carmelita asked for more than any other.

"Tell me about Great-Great-Abuela and the jaguarundi," she begged.

"Oh, Carmelita, you don't want to hear that old story again," Abuela teased.

"I do, I do! *Por favor*, Abuela."

So Abuela told about the hair-raising adventure of her Abuela—Carmelita's Great-Great-Abuela.

Carmelita's favorite part was the description of the jaguarundi. "He was very big, wasn't he, Abuela," she prompted. "Bigger than Papa, who is twice as big as Mamacita."

"Sí, much bigger than Papa or any coatimundi," Abuela confirmed. "He had a flat nose, small round ears, and speckled tan fur. No pretty face markings or tail rings like us."

"How ugly!" Carmelita shivered in horrified delight.

"Very ugly and very dangerous," Abuela agreed. "Many coatimundis became dinner for a hungry jaguarundi back in those days. But, don't worry, *Chiquita*, no one has seen a jaguarundi around here since before I was born."

"What happened to all of them?" Carmelita wondered.

That was a question Abuela could not answer. "Who knows? Maybe they caught a sickness, or maybe humans killed them. Or maybe they just went someplace else."

"Well, it's a good story," Carmelita said. "Tell it again, por favor!"

Carmelita tried to tell the other coatimundis the jaguarundi story, but they wouldn't listen.

"B-o-o-r-r-i-i-n-n-g!" said Maria.

"More boring than your silly questions," Lucia added.

"Hmph! There's no such thing as a jaguarundi!" Tia Louisa scolded.

Mamacita gave Carmelita a hug. "I enjoyed Abuela's stories when I was little, too" she said. "But I don't have time to listen to them now, Chiquita."

Carmelita stopped telling the others about Abuela's stories, but she continued to listen to them. And, sometimes, she pretended jaguarundis were still around and thought about what she would do if she met one. Which, as it turned out, was a very good thing.

One day, Carmelita, Maria and Lucia were gathering Manzanita berries. As they passed a thick sumac bush, a feeble voice called out to them. "Chiquitas, can you help me?" it said.

The kits could see a shadowy figure on the other side of the bush.

"Who are you?" asked Maria.

"I am an old coatimundi from the other side of the mountains. I'm very tired and hungry."

"Why don't you come out where we can see you?" Carmelita asked.

"Carmelita! Don't be rude!" Lucia scolded. "Forgive my hermana," she added, "she is always asking questions."

"So it would seem," the voice said. "I can't come out because I have hurt my leg. You must come to me."

"Poor thing," said Maria. "Of course we'll help you."

Carmelita, curious as always, had tiptoed to the far end of the bush and peeked around it while the others were talking. Instead of an old coatimundi, she saw a creature with a flat nose, little round ears and speckled fur, crouched low and ready to pounce.

"It's a jaguarundi!" she screamed, racing back toward the others, "Run!"

Carmelita led Maria and Lucia to the tallest tree she could see. "Climb!" she told them. "Climb as fast and high as you can!" They scrambled up the tree like stripe-tailed lightning.

"RRWOURR!" the jaguarundi yowled. He shot out from behind the bush and jumped into the tree after them. "I can climb, too, foolish kits!"

Oh, no," Maria wailed. "We're trapped!"

"Keep climbing," Carmelita panted. "Higher!"

Soon, the coatimundis were clinging to the thinnest branches at the very top of the tree with the jaguarundi right below them. He reached for Carmelita. "I'll eat you first, *Senorita Curious!*" he snarled.

Maria and Lucia began to cry. Carmelita held her breath.

Suddenly, just as she'd hoped, the branch the jaguarundi was standing on broke with a loud CRACK. Down he fell, all the way to the ground, landing with a thump and a loud "Oomph!"

"Is—is he dead?" whispered Maria.

"I want Mamacita!" wailed Lucia.

"Wait," Carmelita told them. "Watch."

The jaguarundi sat up with a moan and shook his head. He stared up at the three little coatimundis perched safely out of his reach.

"Aiyee!" he groaned, "My *Abuelo* was right. Coatimundis are hard to catch. I don't like this side of the mountains. I'm going home!"

He climbed to his feet and limped off into the underbrush, never to be seen again.

When they were sure he was gone, Maria, Lucia and Carmelita climbed down and hurried to tell Mamacita, Tia Louisa and Abuela about their narrow escape.

"A jaguarundi!" Tia Louisa exclaimed. "How did you know what to do, Carmelita?"

"Great-Great-Abuela escaped from a jaguarundi by climbing too high for him, just like we did," Carmelita explained. "Abuela told me about it."

"And, if Carmelita hadn't been curious and peeked behind the bush, we wouldn't have known he was a jaguarundi until it was too late," Lucia added.

"So," said Mamacita, "it sounds like Carmelita's curiosity and Abuela's stories saved the day."

"Si! That they did!" agreed Tia Louisa.

From then on, the other coatimundis spent less time being busy and more time being curious, just like Carmelita. And every morning they all gathered and listened to Abuela's stories.

Their favorite story of all was, of course, "Carmelita and the Jaguarundi."

Nature Notes

ABOUT COATIMUNDIS

Coatimundis are a common sight in Central and South America but, in the United States, live in only a few scattered areas of southern Texas, New Mexico and Arizona.

Female coatimundis and their young stay together in groups of four to twenty-five animals. Male coatimundis go off by themselves once they are grown and only show up again during the mating season.

Coatimundis are related to raccoons and, like their northern cousins, eat many kinds of plants, insects and small animals.

A favorite food of coatimundis is the tarantula. These big spiders are very bristly, however, so coatimundis role them around on the ground to rub all their hair off before eating them. (You can see Carmelita's Tia Louisa doing this in one of the pictures.)

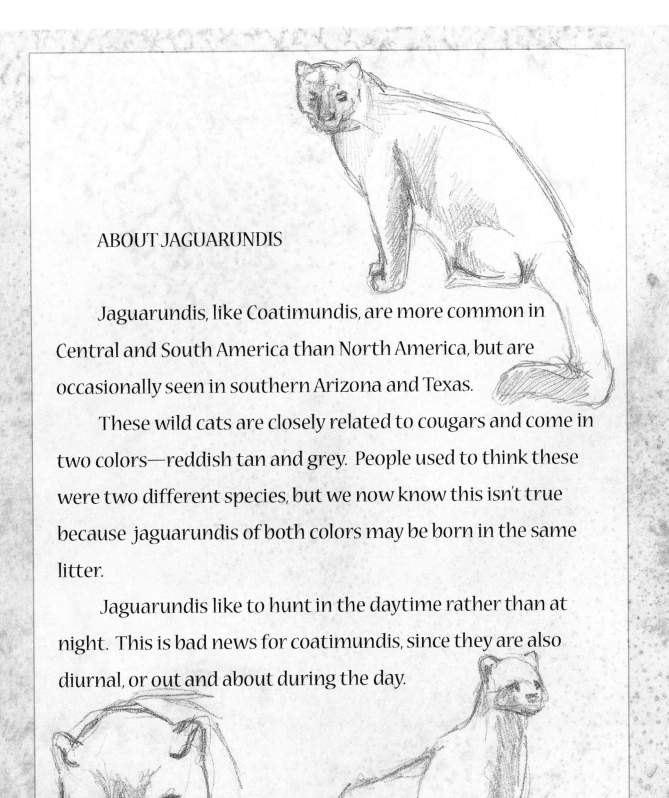

ABOUT JAGUARUNDIS

Jaguarundis, like Coatimundis, are more common in Central and South America than North America, but are occasionally seen in southern Arizona and Texas.

These wild cats are closely related to cougars and come in two colors—reddish tan and grey. People used to think these were two different species, but we now know this isn't true because jaguarundis of both colors may be born in the same litter.

Jaguarundis like to hunt in the daytime rather than at night. This is bad news for coatimundis, since they are also diurnal, or out and about during the day.

There are eight other southwestern animals, birds and insects in this book. See if you can find them all:

Ornate Box Turtles are found east of the Mississippi river in meadowlands from North Dakota to southern Arizona. Their name comes from their colorfully marked domed shell. An Ornate Box Turtle doesn't move around much and may spend its whole life in an area no bigger than a baseball field.

Ornate Box Turtles eat worms, insects, leaves and berries.

A mother Ornate Box Turtle lays one or two clutches of eggs a year. Her newly hatched babies are barely the size of a quarter.

Only male **Chiricahua White Butterflies** are white. The females are orange and are sometimes mistaken for Monarch Butterflies. They are found in isolated areas of southern Arizona and northern Mexico. Chiricahua White Butterfly caterpillars live together in a web or "tent" in the branches of a pine tree. At night, the caterpillars crawl out of their home in a long line to feed.

Chiricahua White Butterflies are very rare. Keep a sharp eye out if you want to be one of the lucky few who manage to spot this pretty insect.

Though widespread in Central America, only a limited number of **Elegant Trogon Birds** migrate to southern Arizona each spring to nest. Thousands of bird watchers travel to the area each year hoping to catch a glimpse of this lovely bird.

Trogon means "gnawer" in Greek and refers to the tough, saw-edged bill the Elegant Trogon uses to gnaw the insects and fruit it eats.

This truly is an elegant bird, especially the males with their bright green heads, scarlet breast feathers and long, graceful tails.

Chiracahua Leopard Frogs used to be a common sight in the streams and rivers of southern Arizona. Nowadays, however, their numbers have dwindled to the point that they are considered a threatened species.

Like all amphibians, these small, spotted frogs hatch from eggs and start out as tadpoles. Their diet consists mainly of insects.

The male Chiracuahua Leopard Frog's mating call sounds just like someone snoring.

Chihuahuan Ravens are one of many species in the bird family corvidae (cor-vid-eye). Their territory stretches from northern Mexico through Arizona and New Mexico to regions of Colorado, Kansas, Oklahoma, and Texas. It used to be called the American White Neck Raven because it's the only American raven species that has white at the base of its black feathers., instead of grey.

Sometimes, Chihuahua Ravens weave the outsides of their nests with thorny twigs or strands of wire, but they always use softer materials on the inside.

Praying Mantises can be found in many parts of the world, including the southern and central United States. The Praying Mantis got its name because of the way it holds its bent forelegs in front of its face as though it is praying. It uses these legs to hold onto its food while it eats it.

The Praying Mantis is sometimes called "the gardener's friend" because it eats many of the insect pests that can ruin garden crops. These odd insects are not very good friends to each other, though, since they also eat other Praying Mantises.

Olive Warblers winter in northern Mexico and spend their summers in the mountains of southern Arizona and New Mexico. Scientists can't decide if they really are warblers or not, so they gave them their own Latin name, Peucedramidae (peh-oo-sed-ram-id-eye).

Olive Warblers eat many kinds of insects and build their nests in the tops of tall conifer trees.

A group of warblers is called a bouquet.

Mexican Spotted Owls have a widespread range, from southern Utah and Colorado to the mountains of Arizona, New Mexico, west Texas, and northern and central Mexico. However, since they prefer to nest only in old-growth forests, their numbers are shrinking.

The Mexican Spotted Owl is a night hunter and eats a wide variety of small rodents, birds, reptiles and insects.

They are one of the few kinds of owls that have dark-colored eyes. Most owls have yellow or orange eyes.

Made in the USA
San Bernardino, CA
09 June 2014